This book is a work of fiction. Any references to historical events, real people, or real places are used fictitiously. Other names, characters, places, and events are products of the author's imagination, and any resemblance to actual events or places or persons, living or dead, is entirely coincidental.

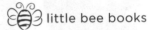 little bee books

An imprint of Bonnier Publishing USA
251 Park Avenue South, New York, NY 10010
Copyright © 2017 by Bonnier Publishing USA
All rights reserved, including the right of reproduction in whole or in part in any form. LITTLE BEE BOOKS is a trademark of Bonnier Publishing USA, and associated colophon is a trademark of Bonnier Publishing USA.

Library of Congress Cataloging-in-Publication Data:
Names: Kent, Jaden, author. | Bodnaruk, Iryna, illustrator.
Title: The great troll quest / by Jaden Kent; illustrated by Iryna Bodnaruk.
Description: First edition. | New York, NY: Little Bee Books, [2017].
Series: Ella and Owen; 5 | Summary: In order to escape from giant trolls, Ella and Owen must grant their wish for puppies, but all the puppies in the land have been taken by an evil Cyclops.
Identifiers: LCCN 2017004960| Subjects: | CYAC: Dragons—Fiction. | Brothers and sisters—Fiction. | Twins—Fiction. | Trolls—Fiction. | Wishes—Fiction. | Adventure and adventurers—Fiction. | Magic—Fiction. | Humorous stories. | BISAC: JUVENILE FICTION / Animals / Mythical. | JUVENILE FICTION / Humorous Stories. | JUVENILE FICTION / Action & Adventure / General.
Classification: LCC PZ7.1.K509 Gre 2017 | DDC [Fic]—dc23
LC record available at https://lccn.loc.gov/2017004960

Printed in the United States of America LB 0717
ISBN 978-1-4998-0474-4 (hc)
First Edition 10 9 8 7 6 5 4 3 2 1
ISBN 978-1-4998-0473-7 (pb)
First Edition 10 9 8 7 6 5 4 3 2 1
littlebeebooks.com
bonnierpublishingusa.com

ELLA AND OWEN

THE GREAT TROLL QUEST

by
Jaden Kent

little bee books

illustrated by
Iryna Bodnaruk

TABLE OF CONTENTS

STUCK ON YOU

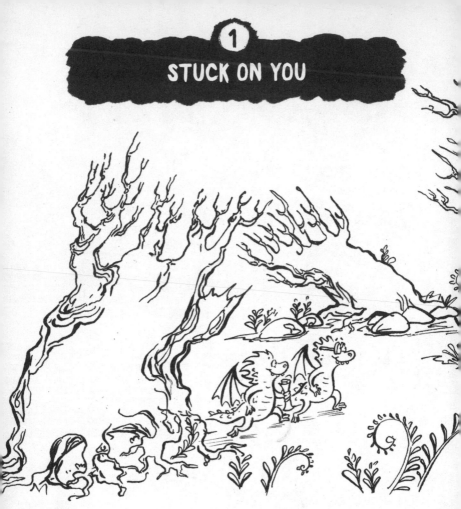

Ella and Owen ran through the forest. Their clawed feet crackled on the dried leaves scattered on the ground.

The Pumpkin King had kept his word. In return for Ella and Owen's help in ending his feud with the witch Rainbow Sparkles, the Pumpkin King had given them a map that would take them out of Terror Swamp and back home to Dragon Patch.

"I think I should look at the map because I read a lot more than you do," Owen explained and grabbed the map from his sister with his claws.

"But I was holding it!" Ella cried. She pulled it away from Owen.

RIP! The map tore in half.
"Now you've done it," Ella accused.

"I should be the one to put it back together," Owen said. "I'm good at puzzles."

4

"No, *I* should put it back together because *you* ripped it apart," Ella replied. She grabbed for the two halves of the map with her claws.

The halves of the map tore in half. The map was now in four pieces.

The dragon twins looked at the pieces. "This is all YOUR fault!" they said to each other.

"We should stop this," Owen suggested. "My dragon math powers aren't strong enough to figure out what half of a half of a half of a map is if we tear it again. I'll put it back together." Owen reached for a sticky slicky slug from the leaf of a nearby prickly stickly tree.

"Gross! Tell me you're not going to eat that," Ella said.

"Not this time. Watch." Owen slid the slug along the edges of the map fragments. Its pasty slime was sticky like glue and Owen got to work connecting the map pieces back together.

"This piece goes here and that one goes there and—argh! Oops," Owen said. "I think I glued a piece of the map to myself."

A square of the map was stuck to Owen's scaly belly. Ella grabbed it and pulled.

"**OWWW!**" Owen yelped. "It's really stuck! That slug slime is really sticky!"

Ella pulled harder. Owen stumbled forward into his sister and their bellies smacked together and got stuck.

Together, they rolled down the path, crashed into a tree stump, and flew into the air.

Map pieces scattered as the dragons plopped to the ground and split apart, landing right at the feet of Dumbdalf the troll.

"Us been looking all over the forest for you two!" Dumbdalf snarled.

Ella and Owen screamed.

Ella grabbed a piece of the map. "Here! We'll go this way!" Ella said, panicked.

Owen and Ella quickly turned away from Dumbdalf and ran into his brother, Dumberdoor, coming down the path.

Owen grabbed another map piece off the ground. "This way!" Owen yelped.

The two dragons flew in the other direction away from Dumberdoor, but Dumbdalf had blocked that escape, too.

"Reading maps hurts my head." Owen handed the map pieces to his sister. "You read it now."

"**Y**ou promised to give wish to trolls when we caught you in Terror Swamp!" Dumberdoor yelled.

"You say you were troll fairies! You owe troll wish now!" Dumbdalf yelled too.

"Welllll . . . we're not really troll fairies," Ella admitted.

"And we can't grant any wishes," Owen added as he started to fly away. "So, I'm glad we had this talk. See you later!"

"No go!" Dumbdalf reached up and grabbed Owen's tail. "Us want wishes!"

"YOWITCH!" Owen yelped. He fluttered back to the ground.

"Not go until us happy," Dumbdalf said.

"Or us gonna have pizza for dinner!" Dumberdoor said.

"Pizza? I love pizza!" Owen clapped. "Is it toadstool pizza with sliced spider eggs?" He happily thumped his tail on the ground.

"No, *you* is the pizza." Dumberdoor tied a napkin around his neck. "Dragon pizza."

"Yuck! I'm definitely my *least* favorite topping," Owen said.

"Wait! Wait! I've got an idea!" Ella interrupted.

"No talk," Dumbdalf said. "Don't like talking dragon pizza."

"No, no, no," Ella continued. "I have a solution that can make you both *very* happy. My brother and I will go on a quest to get you something that you've always wanted!"

"We will?" Owen stared at his sister. She winked at him. Owen understood. "Oh right, we will. It'll be like granting you a wish, but better."

"What have you guys always wanted more than anything else in the whole, wide kingdom?" Ella asked. Dumberdoor was about to answer, but Ella cut him off. "Besides eating dragons."

"Oh," Dumberdoor said. "Then we think."

WHAM! Dumberdoor and Dumbdalf banged their heads together.

"What are you doing?" Owen asked.

"Us is thinking," Dumberdoor said.

"Trolls love thinking," Dumbdalf said.

They whammed their heads together again, then fell backward onto the ground.

"Any ideas yet?" Ella asked.

"Best idea of ever! US WANT A PUPPY!" Dumberdoor and Dumbdalf both shouted.

"A *puppy*?" Owen asked. "You're joking, right?"

"Us never joke when it comes to puppies," Dumberdoor said.

"Puppies is so soft and cute and furry! Us wanna pet it and hug it and love it and name it Clarence Huggybunch the Third!" Dumbdalf added.

"Come on now, you guys!" Ella explained. "Quests are for big, awesome things like magic beans or sparkle swords or powerful rings!"

"Is sparkle sword cute and furry and will it lick troll face?" Dumberdoor asked.

"No, it's a *sword*," Owen replied. "It does sword stuff."

"Then me not interested," Dumberdoor said. "Me want cute puppy."

"Yes, puppy," Dumbdalf added. "Woof! Woof!"

"Oh well. If it's a puppy you guys want, we will go on a quest for one," Ella said. "It'll be—"

"Don't say it . . ." Owen said to Ella.

"A *puppy* quest!" Ella announced.

"We'll get you a puppy and then you two will leave us alone forever. Shake on it." Owen offered a clawed hand to Dumbdalf.

Dumbdalf grabbed Owen's hand, lifting the dragon and shaking him in the air before accidentally flinging him to the ground.

"Shaking a troll's hand hurts more than reading a map," Owen groaned, rubbing his head.

"**W**e look stupid," Ella said.

"Put the cloak on," Owen said. "The humans in this village hate dragons. There's no way we can buy puppies without a disguise."

Ella sat on top of Owen's shoulders. She sighed and wrapped the cloak around them, hiding Owen from sight.

"Now all we have to do is walk through that door and into the store." Owen pointed to the pet shop. "And our puppy quest will be the shortest quest in the history of quests!"

Ella opened the pet shop door and they went inside.

"Welcome, welcome!" a bald man said. He wore a leather apron over his thick body and short legs. "Pick a pet to pet from Pete Popper at Pete Popper's Pets!"

"I need a puppy."

"Check out *this* beautiful little rascal!" Pete exclaimed. He held up a banana with floppy paper ears stuck to it.

"That's just a banana that you taped some ears onto," Ella said.

"No, no, no, it's not," Pete said. "It's a puppy. A thin, yellow puppy." Pete shook the banana. "Ruff! Ruff! See? It's barking!"

"Well, that's not quite the kind of puppy I'm looking for," Ella said.

Pete pointed to a teenage boy in the corner. "Then you'll love that puppy! You won't find anything more adorable than this little guy!"

"I'm not a puppy. I work here!" the teenager in the corner whined. "And it's time for my lunch break!"

Pete leaned in closer to Ella and whispered, "Look, take the boy and I'll throw in the banana puppy and a week's supply of banana puppy food."

Ella shook her head. "No, I want a real puppy, and *only* a real puppy."

Pete sighed, peeled the banana, and took a bite. He tossed the peel on the ground. "I understand. There's only one problem: Pete Popper's Pets doesn't have any puppies."

Ella cried out, "No puppies?!"

"There's not a puppy in this whole town," Pete admitted.

Ella said goodbye and turned to leave. Owen's foot slipped on Pete's banana peel as he lost his balance. Ella and Owen slid across the floor and crashed into a tall stack of pet food, knocking their cloak off.

"I told you to be careful!" Ella and Owen shouted at each other.

"Kittens!" Pete shouted, pointing at them.

"We're *dragons*," Ella sighed.

"Run!" Owen yelled.

The two dragons scampered out of Pete Popper's Pet Store and into the street.

Waiting for them was a group of villagers. They were not happy to see dragons.

PUPPY QUEST GOES WRONG

Pete ran out of his store and pointed at Ella and Owen. "Get those dragons!!!"

Ella and Owen took off down the street. "I'm so scared, my wings won't flap!" Owen said to his sister.

"Then run as fast as your scaly legs can move," she replied.

The dragons raced passed the Build-a-Tool store and the All-You-Can-Meat restaurant. They turned right at the Helmet Depot and were stopped by a tall fence blocking their way. The clerk from Pete's sat on a wooden box in front of it, eating his lunch.

"The dragons are over here!" he yelled.

Pete led the villagers around the corner. Ella and Owen were trapped.

"Ugh. That guy is the worst!" Owen complained.

"We don't want any trouble," Ella said to the villagers.

"Why are you *really* here?" Pete asked.

"Are you going to burn our houses to the ground with your fiery dragon burps?" a villager asked.

"No! We're peaceful dragons . . . on a quest," Ella answered.

"Don't say it," Owen whispered to Ella.

"A *puppy* quest!" Ella announced. Owen groaned.

"Puppies!" one of the villagers sighed. "But . . . they're so cute!"

"And they're cuddly," said another villager.

"Awww, puppies!" the villagers all spoke at once and sighed.

A woman with long blond hair pointed a pitchfork at Ella and Owen. "I declare that these dragons are *good* dragons," she said. "Anyone who wants a puppy cannot be bad, even if it is a dragon."

"Yes, of course!" Pete agreed. The other villagers nodded their heads. "How can we help?"

"Do you know where we can find a puppy to complete our quest?" Owen asked.

"If you want a puppy, you need to go to the most evil, terrible, awful, rotten, really bad place there ever was. . . ." Pete said, pointing toward the horizon.

The two dragons turned and saw that he was pointing to a beautiful, flower-covered mountain with a rainbow over it.

"Um . . . is the most evil, terrible, awful, rotten, really bad place there ever was *behind* the beautiful, flower-covered mountain with a rainbow over it?" Ella asked.

"No! It *is* the beautiful, flower-covered mountain with a rainbow over it," Pete replied. "Don't let that rainbow fool you. It's a really nasty place!"

"It kinda looks like fun," Owen said.

"No!" Pete said. "A creature that lives in a cave in the mountain there took all our puppies away!"

"And does this nasty place have a name?" Ella asked.

"Oh yeah! It's got an evil, terrible, awful, rotten, really bad name!" Pete said.

"Like the Mountain of Doom?" Owen asked. "Or Haunted Mountain? Or . . ."

"No!" Pete replied. "We call it Mount Cuddle Muffin!"

THE MOST EVIL, TERRIBLE, AWFUL, ROTTEN, REALLY BAD PLACE EVER

Ella and Owen found themselves at the base of Mount Cuddle Muffin in their quest to find a puppy for the trolls.

"This place doesn't look so evil," Owen said, looking around.

"Or terrible," Ella added.

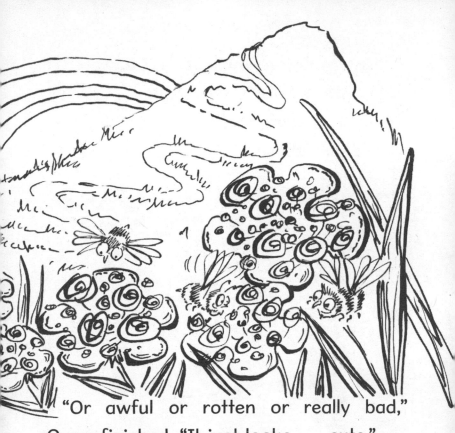

"Or awful or rotten or really bad,"
Owen finished. "It just looks . . . cute."

Owen was right. Mount Cuddle Muffin
was by far the cutest place in the world.
It was covered in cute flowers. Cute
sunshine beamed down from cute clouds
and made the cutest rainbow ever.

Ella and Owen flew up and discovered a sign a little farther up the mountain. A skull and crossbones made from candy canes was stuck above a warning scrawled in bold letters:

HERE BE MOUNT CUDDLE MUFFIN, HOME TO THE MOST EVIL, TERRIBLE, AWFUL, ROTTEN, REALLY BAD CREATURES IN THE KINGDOM! BE YE WARNED TO TURN BACK NOW OR NEVER BE HEARD FROM AGAIN!

Owen looked around, but all he could see was a pack of soft, fuzzy bunnies peacefully hopping about in the heather.

"The sign is probably just to keep the villagers away," Owen said. He flew over to the nearest bunny and gently petted its soft white fur. "I mean, how could something so cute be evil, terrible, awful, rotten, *or* really bad?!"

"HISSS!" The bunny bared its sharp fangs. Its eyes glowed red.

The other bunnies stopped nibbling carrots. Their eyes glowed red as well. They hissed and charged at Owen, snapping at him with their sharp fangs.

"Ah! Get these evil, terrible, awful, rotten, really bad, but-still-super-cute bunnies away from me!" Owen shouted, panicking.

Ella pulled two large carrots from the ground and threw one to Owen. "Here! Use this!"

"Thanks, but I'm not hungry!" Owen yelled and yanked his tail away from one bunny's chomping fangs.

"Don't eat it, fire-for-brains! Fight them with it!" Ella yelled.

Owen held the large carrot like a sword and swung it wildly at the evil bunnies.

"Back! Back! Back, you evil, terrible, awful, rotten, really bad bunnies!" Owen said, keeping the carrot between the bunnies and him.

"Keep swinging!" Ella said. "They're starting to run away!"

Unfortunately, the bunnies were *not* running away. They were just making space for two huge, drooling, growling bunnies that were coming up from behind them.

"This is *not* good!" Owen said.

"CHOMP! CHOMP!" The two large bunnies bit into Ella and Owen's pretend swords, leaving the dragons with nothing but carrot stems to defend themselves.

"Can't we just go get the trolls a pet goldfish instead?!" Owen asked as he and Ella ran for their lives with the giant, evil, terrible, awful, rotten, really bad bunnies nipping at their tails in pursuit.

"**Q**uick! Into that cave!" Ella shouted to Owen. "We can use our dragon vision and lose them in the dark!"

"What if they have evil, terrible, awful, rotten, really bad bunny vision and can see in the dark, too?" Owen asked.

"Then I guess the trolls won't be getting their puppy, will they?" Ella replied.

Ella and Owen flew quickly into the dark cave. It smelled like an old shoe and was damper than an ogre's armpits. The two dragons landed behind a large rock and hid.

"Look around and see if they're following us," Owen said. He folded his wings around his body as tightly as he could.

"You look," Ella replied. Her tail was nervously thumping on the ground.

"This was your idea," Owen reminded her. "*You* look."

Ella snorted dragon smoke through her nostrils and peeked out from behind the rock.

"We're safe," she said, sighing. "They didn't follow us in here."

"This is bad!" Owen whined. "Really, really bad!"

"How could evil rabbits with glowing red eyes and fangs not following us into a cave be *bad*?!" Ella asked.

"If something evil, terrible, awful, rotten, and really bad won't chase you into a cave, it's because something even more eviler, terribler, awfuler, rottener, and really badderer is in the cave waiting for you!" Owen explained.

"Are your wings on backward?" Ella laughed. "They didn't follow us into the cave because they were clearly afraid of me."

"If they were afraid of you, then why were *you* running away from *them*?" Owen asked.

"All part of my awesome plan," Ella said. "Which totally worked." Ella got out from behind the rock and flew deeper into the cave. "Now let's go find a puppy."

The two dragons flew deeper and deeper into the darkness and finally came to a large area where they found the villagers' pet puppies happily playing and rolling about.

"Those must be the villagers' puppies!" Owen said.

"Now *these* guys are cute!" Ella said, crouching down to play with some of the puppies.

"Can we please just grab one and get out of here before their eyes start glowing red or something?" Owen asked, nervously looking around the cave. "Remember what the villagers said? Their puppies were taken by a creature living in the cave!"

"You worry too much," Ella replied.

"And you don't worry enough!" Owen warned.

But before Owen could explain to his sister that he worried just the perfect amount, he felt someone watching them. The two dragons looked up to see a very big Cyclops blocking their exit.

"Okay. *Now* I'm worried!" Ella gulped.

YOU GOTTA BE KITTEN ME!

"**K**ittens!" the Cyclops joyfully cheered.

"CYCLOPS!" Ella and Owen both screamed.

The Cyclops grabbed Ella and Owen and gave them a crushing hug. The Cyclops put them down and tossed them a large ball of yarn. "Kittens play!"

"We're not kittens," Ella explained. "We're dragons, and dragons do not play with balls of yarn."

"This is awesome!" Owen rolled around on the ground with the ball of yarn. "I've gotta get one of these things for my bedroom!"

"Boy kitten is playing with yarn so he must be a kitten," the Cyclops said and crossed his arms. He stood almost eighteen feet tall and wore a belt of crocodile teeth wrapped around a tunic made from the hides of a bear, a deer, and at least one cow. He had snakeskin sandals on his dirty feet, a small patch of brown hair atop his mostly bald head and, like all Cyclopes, had only one eye just above his nose.

"Maybe you can help us, Mr. Cyclops, sir?" Ella nervously asked.

"Do you need help finding more yarn to play with, kitten?" the Cyclops asked.

"No, because, uh, like I said, we're *not* kittens," Ella began. "We're dragons and we're on a—"

"Don't say it . . ." Owen said to Ella.

"*Puppy* quest!" Ella announced.

Ella carefully tiptoed over to the puppies on her claws. "So, would it be okay if we kinda, you know, *took* one of these puppies?"

"Kittens want puppies?! Hahahahaha!"
The Cyclops burst out with laughter
that shook the cave walls.
"That is funniest thing
I have ever heard!
Kittens don't
like puppies!
Kittens like
mice, and
puppies are
not mice, so
kittens should
not like them!"

"We could trade
you!" Owen said.
"How'd you like some
crazy rabbits with
glowing red eyes and really,
really sharp fangs?"

"Not want that," the Cyclops said and turned his back to them.

"What if we gave you a big pile of gold for one of the puppies?" Ella asked.

The Cyclops turned to face them, his lone eye wide with excitement.

"Is pile of gold cute and furry and will it play fetch and lick my face?" the Cyclops asked.

"No, it's just *gold*," Owen replied.

"Then I'm not interested," the Cyclops replied. "I want cute puppies."

A frustrated Ella blew a puff of dragon smoke from her nose. "But!"

"No more talking kittens and their strange talking-kitten questions." The Cyclops picked up Owen and Ella and placed them in a cage, closing the door behind them. "This is your new talking-kitten home forever and ever and ever and for a very long time after that, too."

Ella and Owen both grabbed the cage's bars. They were trapped!

"Well, the good news is, I won't have to clean my room anymore." Owen sighed.

"We can't stay here for the rest of our lives!" Ella said. "I start dragon stunt flying school next month!"

"At least he gave us a ball of yarn," Owen said and happily batted the yarn around the cage.

"That gives me an idea!" Ella excitedly flapped her wings. "Oh, Mr. Cyclops, sir! Me and my yarn-headed brother were wondering if you'd let us out of the cage so we have more room to play with the yarn?" Ella asked.

"Okay, talking kitten-with-scales-and-not-fur," the Cyclops said and opened the cage.

"Any chance you've got more yarn?" Ella asked.

"Oh, sure, talking kitten-with-wings. It's a little-known fact that Cyclopes love to knit!" The Cyclops grabbed a basket behind him and dumped more balls of yarn on top of Owen.

"ACK!" Owen yelped as a giant yarn ball squished him.

Ella shoved the big ball of yarn off of him. "Thanks, Sis," he groaned.

"Want to play a game with us?" Ella asked.

"Yay! I like games!" The Cyclops clapped. "My favorite is Chase Puny, Annoying Villagers with Giant Club!"

"Do what I do!" Ella whispered to Owen.

Ella and Owen picked up some of the colorful strands of thread and flew circles around the Cyclops, wrapping up his legs, arms, and body with the yarn. After a dizzying number of loops, the Cyclops was tightly bound from head to toe with yarn.

"Hey! I can't move!" the Cyclops said. "Does that mean I won or lost?"

"That means you won!" Ella cheered.

"Yay! What'd I win? What'd I win?" the eager Cyclops asked.

"You won us taking all the puppies and getting outta here," Owen replied.

The Cyclops squinted his one eye as he thought. "That's not a very good prize," he said and started to cry.

"Is the Cyclops . . . *crying*?" Ella asked Owen in disbelief.

"It's probably just tears of joy for winning the game. Let's go!" Owen hastily pushed Ella toward the exit.

"We can't leave. I want to find out what's wrong." Ella spun away from her brother and flew over to the weeping Cyclops.

"Aw, dragon scales," Owen sighed. "Looks like I'm gonna spend the rest of my life as a kitten."

"Why are you crying?" Ella asked the Cyclops.

"Because no one wants to be friends with a one-eyed Cyclops who lives in a cave surrounded by very mean, but somehow still cute, bunnies," the Cyclops sobbed.

"And so you took the puppies from the village so you'd have friends?" Ella asked.

"Yeah. I was lonely. And now that you're taking the puppies away, I'll be alone again." The Cyclops started to sob even louder.

Owen's wings sagged. "Boy, I never thought I'd feel so bad for escaping from a Cyclops who was trying to keep me as a pet kitten."

"We'll just have to find the trolls a goldfish and tell them that we failed on our puppy quest," Ella said.

"Or, wait . . . either I bumped my head and it hurts . . . or I just had an idea!" Owen said.

"*You* have an idea?" Ella asked.

"I know! Crazy, huh?" Owen said, smiling.

After bringing all the puppies back to the village, Ella and Owen returned to the trolls' camp where an excited Dumberdoor and Dumbdalf greeted them.

"Where's us puppy?!" Dumberdoor asked.

"We couldn't find you a puppy, but we got you something even better!" Ella said to the trolls.

"TWO PUPPIES! YAAAAAY!" Dumbdalf happily shouted.

"No, no, no," Owen said. "We got you *zero* puppies."

"Zero puppies! Yaaaaaay!" Dumberdoor cheered, then looked to Dumbdalf and asked, "Zero puppies is more than two, right?"

"Me not sure," Dumbdalf replied. "Me not good with spelling."

"We got you a new *friend*," Ella said as the Cyclops timidly came out from his hiding place.

"Ooooh! Me like friends! They're very delicious!" Dumbdalf said.

"You don't *eat* them!" Owen replied.

"Then what good is they?" Dumberdoor asked.

"Don't look at me," Ella said, turning to Owen. "This was your idea!"

"You hang out with them and play with them and . . . and . . . tell them your hopes and dreams!" Owen said to the trolls.

"Me hope us can eat him!" Dumbdalf said, licking his lips.

"And me *dream* us can eat him!" Dumberdoor added.

"Or, um, mmm, maybe, um, we can play with *yarn* instead?" the Cyclops asked and shyly offered a ball of yarn to the two trolls.

"Us love yarn!" Dumbdalf clapped his hands. "Us can play like kittens!"

Dumbdalf rolled the yarn ball to Dumberdoor, who rolled it to the Cyclops, who rolled it back to Dumbdalf.

"Us like new friend!" Dumbdalf said. "Us will name him George!"

"George?!" the Cyclops said with a gasp. "That is such a very good, favorite name and it is *so* much better than the name I have now!"

"What name is that?" Ella asked.

"The Horrible, Ugly, Stinky, One-Eyed Monster that Lives in the Scary Cave," George the Cyclops answered before adding, "I did not make it up myself, in case you were wondering."

"Thank you for bringing me new friends,"
George said and gave Owen and Ella a
big, crushing hug.

"You're welcome," Owen groaned.

As George the Cyclops, Dumberdoor, and Dumbdalf happily played, Ella and Owen flapped their wings, lifted off the ground, and took their leave.

"Do you really think it's a good idea to bring trolls and a Cyclops together?" Ella asked.

"Nope, but it beats us being eaten," Owen replied, looking at his sister, which caused him to not see a swamp tree branch directly in front of him. He smacked right into it and crashed to the ground.

Ella swooped down to help him, but the moment she landed, the ground gave way beneath them both. The two dragons tumbled down into a long, dark, twisting tunnel.

They fell, bouncing about, too dizzy to recover their footing. "OUCH!

OOCH!

EEK!"
Owen grunted.

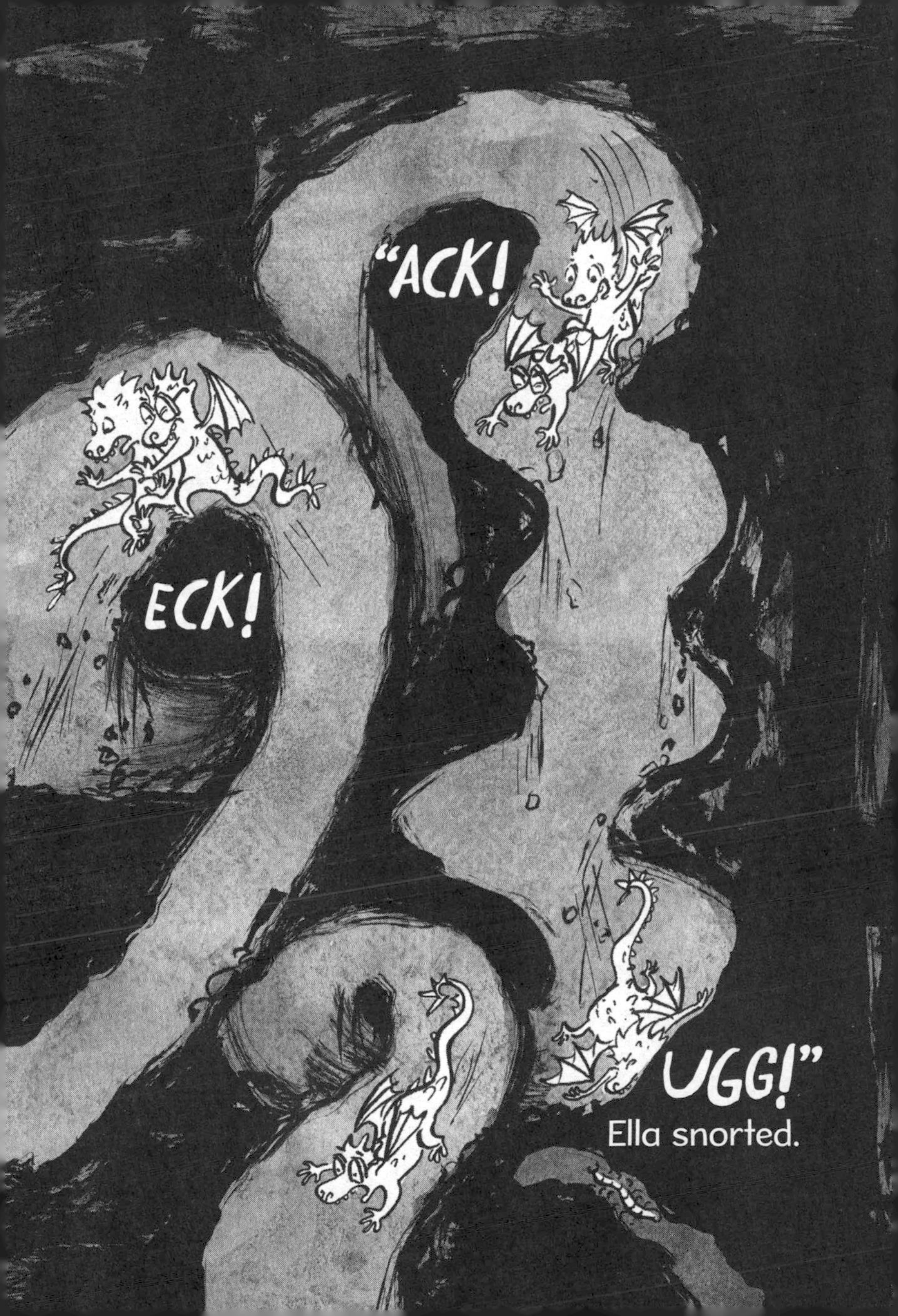
"ACK!
ECK!
UGG!"
Ella snorted.

THUD! The two dragons finally hit the ground in the bottom of a dark, wet, underground cavern.

"Do you know where we are?" Owen asked as he shook the mud from his wings, looking around.

"No. And I have no idea how to get out of here," Ella answered.

GULP!

Read on for a sneak peek from the
sixth book in the Ella and Owen series!

BOOK 6
ELLA AND OWEN
DRAGON SPIES!
by Jaden Kent
illustrated by Iryna Bodnaruk

1

THE CAVE OF DARKNESS

Dragon twins Ella and Owen plopped onto the dark, cold ground of the cave.

"This is all your fault!" Ella said.

"How is this my fault?" Owen replied.

"If you hadn't hit your head on that branch, I wouldn't have tried to help you and we wouldn't have fallen into this dark cave," Ella said. "I think I bent my tail."

Ella felt a root poking out from the

side of the cavern. She lit it with her fire breath. Light flickered around the room.

Owen screamed, "Noooo!"

Tall, creepy, hand-carved wooden statues of fierce warrior dwarves holding shovels lined the large underground chamber.

"I don't want to see this!" Owen patted on the root with his tail to put out the fire. The chamber was dark again.

"Don't be such a baby," an annoyed Ella said. She lit the root again.

"Nooooo!" Owen screamed, able to see the dwarf statues again. He blew out the flame. The chamber was dark once more.

"Would you *please* stop doing that?" Ella snapped.

"Not until those creepy statues go away!" Owen replied.

Ella took a deep breath, ready to light the root one more time, but she stopped and let out a puff of steam instead.

BA-DOOM-BOOM!

"Did you hear that?" she asked.

"Hear what?" Owen replied.

BA-DOOM-BOOM-BOOM!

"That!" Ella pointed down the dark cavern.

BA-DOOM-BOOM-BA-DOOM!

"It sounds like drums. And drums mean that someone down that dark tunnel is going to come out and try to eat us," Owen explained. "So let's get out of here!"

"Let's go check it out," Ella urged.

"Oh no," replied Owen. He shook his head. "Drums being played in a dark, underground cavern never ends in anything good."

"Don't be such a scaly baby," Ella said. "I'm going to go take a look. It might be a way out of here." She fluttered her wings and flew toward the sound of the drums.

Owen sighed and followed her. "This will only end in tears," he said. "Probably mine."

The two dragons flew down the long tunnel. They entered a well-lit chamber where two bearded dwarves danced in a circle. A third bearded dwarf pounded on two short tribal drums. The dwarves' hairy bare feet poked out from underneath blue overalls. Their scraggly hair needed a comb. They each had large noses that took up most of their faces. The drumming dwarf stopped playing and pointed to Ella and Owen at the entrance.

"Intruders!" he shouted.

"Score update!" Owen told Ella. "Evil drums: one. My sister who never listens to me: zero!"

"Get them!" The three dwarves charged toward Ella and Owen.